For Adam—and the atom, and other
necessary elements. —S.G.B.

Tricycle Press

an imprint of Ten Speed Press

P.O. Box 7123

Berkeley, California 94707

www.tricyclepress.com

Design by Randall Heath
Typeset in GenericaCondensed
The illustrations in this book were rendered in mixed digital media

Library of Congress Cataloging-in-Publication Data

Brown, Stephanie Gwyn, 1963–

Professor Aesop's the crow and the pitcher / illustrated and interpreted by Stephanie Gwyn Brown   p. cm.

Summary: A clever crow uses the scientific method to get a drink from a nearly empty pitcher in this
adaptation of a fable from Aesop. Includes an explanation of the scientific method's six steps.

ISBN-13: 978-1-58246-087-1 / ISBN-10: 1-58246-087-6

[1. Fables. 2. Folklore. 3. Science—Methodology.] I. Title.

PZ8.2.B75 Cr 2003   398.2—dc21   2002014331

Printed in Singapore
First Tricycle Press printing, 2003
4 5 6 7 8 — 10 09 08 07 06

Professor Aesop's

THE CROW AND THE PITCHER

illustrated and interpreted by

Stephanie Gwyn Brown

Tricycle Press
Berkeley/Toronto

A thirsty crow, half-dead from desert heat,

came upon a water pitcher.

When he lowered his beak
into the mouth of the pitcher,
the crow discovered very little water.

He could not reach
far
enough
down
to take a drink.

PROBLEM:

BEAK
(too short)

PITCHER
(too narrow)

WATER
(too low)

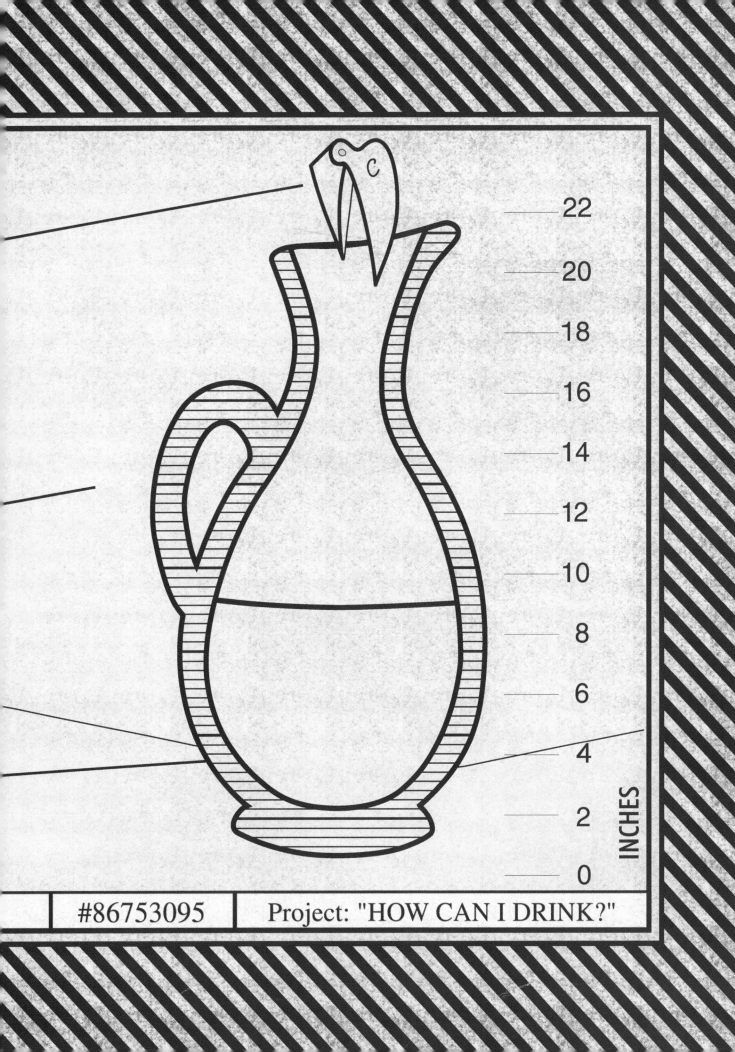

22

20

18

16

14

12

10

8

6

4

2

0

INCHES

#86753095   Project: "HOW CAN I DRINK?"

After several attempts,

he
gave up
in despair.

bird's brain

GENIUS ALERT

Then he got an

IDEA!

(drawn from information and inspiration)

DETERMINATION

low high

Danger

High

Mild

Low

THIRST-O-METER

AMBIENT TEMPERATURE

VERY HOT

HOT

WARM

COOL

COLD

He plucked a pebble from the ground
and dropped it into the pitcher.

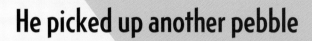

He picked up another pebble

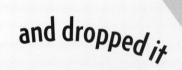

and dropped it

into the pitcher.

PEBBLE INDICATOR
0 0 0 2

Then another.

and another.

At last,
many pebbles later,
the water rose near the top.

DETERMINATION

THIRST-O-METER

Danger
High
Mild
Low

AMBIENT TEMPERATURE

VERY HOT
HOT
WARM
COOL
COLD

PEBBLE INDICATOR

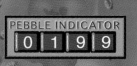

low high

DETERMINATION

Danger

High

Mild

Low

THIRST-O-METER

AMBIENT TEMPERATURE

VERY HOT

HOT

WARM

COOL

COLD

After dropping in a
few more pebbles,

and saved his life.

THE SCIENTIFIC METHOD ACCORDING TO CROW

2.

Gather up the facts to find the answer to that question.

Crow inspects,

checks, kicks

and pecks!

1.

Question!
Question?
Start out with a
question!

"How can I drink?"

"Now time to think."

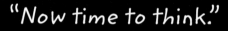

PEBBLES

THOMAS ALVA
EDISON
1847-1931
*"Genius is 1%
inspiration &
99%
Perspiration..."*

WATER LEVEL

PEBBLES

5.
Review the results to get a sense of your success.

3.
Form a hypothesis, an educated guess.

SCIENTIFIC TIMES

SCIENCE AWARDS

CROW WINS
SCIENTIST OF THE YEAR
WITH
WATER DISPLACEMENT
THEORY

6.
Be a true scientist and share it with the rest.

$$D = \frac{M}{V}$$

300 ml
250
200
150
100
50

400ml

400ml
250
200
150
100
50

400ml
300 ml
250
200
150
100
50

4.
Then tackle the experiment and put it to the test.